An American is a person who isn't afraid to criticize the President . . . but is always polite to traffic cops.

* * *

What do they call the Gary Hart scandal?
   Tailgate!

* * *

You look at the news every day; there's rape, muggings, strikes.
Maybe the Indians should have had stricter immigration laws.

* * *

What's the definition of Italian foreplay?
   "Honey, I'm home!"

* * *

What's a Polish wedding proposal?
   "You're what?"

* * *

An old Jewish woman is sitting on the beach and a man walks by and she says, "My, you're awfully pale." And the man says, "as a matter of fact, I am." The woman asks why. The man tells her that he's been in prison. The woman says, "So you're single!"

#3 JOKING OFF

#3
JOKING OFF

JOHNNY LYONS

PaperJacks LTD.

TORONTO   NEW YORK

AN ORIGINAL

PaperJacks

#3 JOKING OFF

PaperJacks LTD

330 STEELCASE RD. E., MARKHAM, ONT. L3R 2M1
210 FIFTH AVE., NEW YORK, N.Y. 10010

First edition published December 1987

This original PaperJacks edition is printed from brand-new plates made from newly set, clear, easy-to-read type. No part of this book may be reproduced or transmitted in any form or by any means, electronic or mechanical, including photography, recording, or any information storage or retrieval system, without permission in writing from the publisher.

ISBN 0-7701-0714-1
Copyright © 1987 by Lion Entertainment, Inc.
All rights reserved
Printed in the U.S.A

This book is dedicated to all the people who love jokes! Particularly to my many friends, business associates, and acquaintances who have generously shared their jokes with me over the years.

These include:

Robin, who corrected my spelling errors for years; that very special hot little honey of mine who kept supplying Johnny boy with joke after joke, week after week, month after month . . . thanks, baby; to Doc; Johnny Zero; John E. or S., depending on what kind of mood he or you are in; Raul; Darwin the Magnificent; Willard Wombato of the weird club; Ira the answering-service man; Pinky; Foul Al, who will always remain the foulest; and Yvonne; and to my wonderful secretaries, Pee Wee aka Virginia B.; and Rose B., and of course to my Mickey; Zaqum; and big bad Bill for all those jokes; hah hah hah to all!

TABLE OF CONTENTS

Part One: Sex, Drugs, & Rock 'n' Roll ... 1
Part Two: Food Jokes! 29
              The Worst Diet You Ever Read! 31
Part Three: Hollyweird! 41
              Jokes about Hollywood, Los Angeles, and the Entertainment Industry 43
Part Four: Ethnic Jokes 51
              Black Jokes 53
              Gay Jokes 57
              Italian Jokes 63
              Jewish Jokes 67
              Polish Jokes 71
              Miscellaneous Ethnic Jokes .. 79
Part Five: Conceited Lines 87
Part Six: Very Sick and Extremely Sick Jokes 93
Part Seven: Some Popular Sayings 115

Part One

SEX, DRUGS, & ROCK 'N' ROLL

A man walked into a bar and spotted a very attractive woman. He approached her and said, "Hey, I'd like to buy you a drink." The woman agreed, and he bought her a drink and they began to make small talk. "I think you're very attractive," the man said. "What are you doing when you leave the bar?" The woman said, "I'd like you to know that I'm a lesbian, buddy." The man said, "Well, I'm sorry, ma'am, but, what is a lesbian?" The woman replied, "To give you an example, do you see that beautiful blonde over there with the voluptuous breasts, the cleavage, and the long legs? Well, I'd like to go over there and put my head between her legs and chew her bush all night long!" The man chimed in, "Well, ma'am, I guess I'm a lesbian, too!"

A lady has leg trouble, so she goes to the doctor and he tells her to do some leg raises. She goes back home and does some leg raises. She and her husband are then in the mood for sex. She goes upstairs and starts raising her legs up and down. She has her legs up, and she gets stuck! Her husband comes in the room, and he says, "Hey, comb your hair, brush your teeth. You look like an asshole!"

* * *

An Indian goes into a bar in Virginia with a bottle of whiskey, a bucket full of bullshit, a double-barrel shotgun, and a dead pussycat. He's sitting at the bar, takes a sip out of the bottle of whiskey, and shoots a hole in the bucket full of bullshit, and he takes a bite out of the dead pussycat. He does it four or five times before the bartender asks him what the hell he's trying to do. So, before he answers, he does it again. He takes a sip out of the bottle of whiskey, he shoots a hole in the bucket of bullshit, and he takes a bite out of the dead pussycat! The bartender asks him again what on earth he is doing. He replies, "Me want to be like white man. Me want to get drunk, shoot the bullshit, and eat pussy!"

* * *

Why can't a witch have babies?
   Because her husband has a Hallo-ween!
Why can't a pencil have babies?
   Because her husband has a rubber tip!
Why can't a gypsy have babies?
   Because her husband has crystal balls!

Three white men are off exploring an African jungle. All of a sudden, they get captured by a tribe of Ungawas. They separate the three men and ask the first one, "Do you prefer death, or do you prefer Ungawa?" And the white man replied, "Well, I prefer Ungawa. It sounds much better than death." The tribe leader turns around and tells his tribe, "Ungawa!" They proceed to take the man to the hut, and a hundred tribe members give it to him, right up the shit shoot. So they go up to the second white guy and ask him the same question. He replies, "Well, I prefer Ungawa," without even guessing what happened to the first guy. They take him to the back of the hut as well, and they ram his rectum also. The third guy gets asked the very same question, "Do you prefer death, or do you prefer Ungawa?" And he tells the tribe leader, "I prefer death — kill me!" So the tribe leader turns around and he tells his tribe, "Death by Ungawa!" So even the last man gets fucked, any way you put it!!

* * *

What's the difference between a pussy and a cunt?

A pussy is an adorable creature that is warm and fuzzy. A cunt is what wears it.

* * *

A male friend of mine had severe headaches. He was in excruciating pain, so he went to the doctor. The doc gave him a thorough exam, and said, "Well, I have some bad news for you. In order to overcome these headaches you'll have to be castrated." The man got very upset, and asked, "Are you sure there's nothing else we can do?" The doctor assured him that castration was his only option. "Look, Doc, I can't decide about this right now," the man said. So he went home and thought about it for a week, but the bad headaches continued. They got so bad he couldn't even go to work. So he okayed the operation.

The doctor operated and the man felt just great. He decided to go on a binge — planned for a trip to Europe and went out to buy a wardrobe. He arrived at an expensive tailor's, who said, "Wait, I know your size. You're a size 42 jacket, a size 36 pants, a 16½ shirt, and size 36 underwear." "Wow," replied the man, "you're exactly right, except that I wear size 34 underwear." "No way," said the tailor. "But I've been buying and wearing size 34 for years!" exclaimed the man. The tailor replied, "Well, if you were wearing size 34 underwear, you'd be having such unbearable headaches you wouldn't know what to do!"

* * *

A woman goes to Dr. Maserati. As the doctor examines her, he says, "Ma'am, I can't believe my eyes. Your right breast is three times as big as your left." She says, "My husband loves to sleep with one of them in his mouth." Dr. Maserati says, "I sleep with my wife the same way, but hers are normal." The woman says, "I guess you don't have twin beds."

A hawk is out flying around, looking for a little action because he's feeling horny. He sees a flock of birds, lands, scores with one of them, and soars away, feeling so great that he starts to sing, "I've just had a dove, and I'm in love!" After a while, the thrill wears off, and he's on the prowl again. He lands again, has his fun, and once again soars away, singing, "I've just had a lark, and I feel a spark!" A little while later, ready again for love, he sees a flock of ducks on a lake. He lands, does his thing, and sings happily, "I've just had a duck, and what a fuck!" But this time, the duck says, "You've just made a mistake, I'm a drake!"

* * *

An eighty-year-old man marries a forty-year-old woman. All of the man's friends want to know how the honeymoon was. The old man tells them it was fantastic and that he has married a forty-year-old virgin, and that the sex was the best he's ever had. The woman's friends also question her about the honeymoon. The young bride tells her girlfriends that she's married an eighty-year-old sex maniac. She also tells them that he screwed her brains out, but never allowed her to take her panty hose off.

* * *

Did you hear about the new S&M series premiering this fall? It's called "Gag Me and Lace Me."

A guy walks into a bar with his octopus. He sits down, orders himself a draft, and boasts, "My octopus is the most musically talented octopus in the world. He can play any instrument." The bartender has nothing else to do, so he bets the man $100 that he can find an instrument that the octopus can't play. The man accepts the bet, and the bartender presents a trombone for the octopus to play. Lo and behold, the octopus wraps his talented tentacles around the trombone and knocks out a flawless rendition of a really difficult piece. This goes on between the bartender and the octopus, and the beast plays a flute, clarinet, saxophone, and guitar flawlessly. Finally, when the bartender presents the octopus with a bagpipe, the performance is stalled. "What's the matter with your octopus, buddy? Where's the 'Highland Fling'?" The man keeps his cool and answers, "Don't worry. As soon as he figures out that he can't fuck it, he'll play it!"

* * *

What do you get when you cross a woman and a computer microchip?

A cunt that will do anything!

* * *

A very sexual woman comes before Judge Daniels, who reprimands her. "Mrs. Jones, we have witnesses that claim you are an active, oversexed nymphomaniac! What have you got to say — Hey what happened to my gavel?"

A man gets his penis amputated in a car accident, so they graft on a baby elephant's trunk. He's very shy about the whole thing, and invites this woman out to dinner in a very posh restaurant. All the waiters are in tuxedos, there's candlelight, soft music — it's all very elegant. All of a sudden, the baby elephant's trunk scoots out of the man's pants, scoots across the table and grabs a roll out of the basket, and scoots back down. The girl sees this, but she's not quite sure she saw what she thinks she saw. So, a few minutes later they're talking, and the baby elephant's trunk scoots out again, grabs another roll, and scoots back down. This time the girl exclaims, "Oh, my God, what was that?" The man hems and haws and finally admits to the fact that he had his penis amputated in a car crash and that he had a baby elephant's trunk grafted on instead. "That's great!" says the woman. "Can you make it scoot across the table again?" The man replies, "I would, but I don't think my ass can take another roll!"

* * *

A very successful executive is fed up with the corporate world and decides to become a farmer. So he decides to move out west. When he arrives, he goes to a livestock sale and asks to buy some animals and asks the salesman to sell him a rooster. The salesman says, "Sir, out here we call them cocks."

So the man says, "Give me a cock!"

The man then asks if he has a hen.

The salesman replies, "Out here we call 'em pullets."

So the man says, "Give me a pullet!"

The man next asks, "What else you got?" The salesman says he has a jackass, but explains to him that sometimes he stops dead in his tracks, but all the man has to do is rub his ears when he does this and he'll move right along. So the man leaves the livestock sale on the jackass with the cock and the pullet on the back of the jackass. Sure enough, the man proceeds for a few miles, and the jackass stops dead in his tracks. The man is perplexed because he's forgotten what to do when this happens. Suddenly an old woman appears and asks him if she can do anything to help him. The man then remembers that he is supposed to scratch the jackass behind the ears, so he says to the woman, "Yes, you can help me. Would you hold my cock and pullet, while I scratch my ass!"

* * *

A bear went up to his mother and said, "Mother, what kind of bear am I?" The mother replied, "You are a polar bear, and you are my son." The little baby bear said again, "Mother, what kind of a bear am I?" The mother said again, "You are a polar bear and you are my son." The baby bear said, "Mother, are you sure that I'm not a brown bear?" Momma said, "No, you're a polar bear and you're my son." The baby bear said, "Are you sure that I'm not a grizzly bear?" The momma said, "What are you asking all these questions for? You are a polar bear and you are my son." So the little baby bear went over to the the papa bear and said, "Papa, am I a panda bear?" The papa replied, "No, you're a polar bear and you are my son." The baby pushed on. "Are you sure I'm not a koala bear?" Papa replied, "No, you are a polar bear and you are my son. Why are you asking all these questions?" Baby bear answered, "Because I'm cold!"

* * *

Two men are talking to each other, and one says to the other, "Do you talk to your wife while you're having sexual relations?" The other man replies, "I would if I could reach the telephone!"

* * *

A husband and wife throw a very lavish Halloween party, and everyone comes to the party extremely decked out. One woman is dressed as Cleopatra, and it takes four men to carry her around in her litter. Another man is dressed as Count Dracula. A naked woman appears, too. The male host says, "You look lovely tonight, but who are you supposed to be?" The woman says, "Adam." The host replies, "But you don't have a cock!" The woman says, "That's no problem. I'll find one!"

* * *

A seventy-year-old man married a beautiful thirty-five-year-old woman. One day the young wife found out that her husband was fooling around with a woman who was sixty-five years old. She puts up with it, until one day she said to her husband, "Here I am. I'm young and beautiful and I thought we had a wonderful life together. Now I find out you're fooling around with a woman who's sixty-five! What on earth has she got that I haven't got?" The man replied, "Patience!"

* * *

A drunk was walking on the street with one foot on the curb and one foot in the gutter. A cop stopped him and said, "I've got to take you in, you're totally drunk." The guy said, "Officer, are you absolutely sure I'm drunk?" The officer said, "Yes, you're drunk." The drunk says, "Thank goodness. I thought I was a cripple!"

* * *

A bartender has a bull mastiff killer dog. Someone comes into the bar and the bartender brags, "I have the deadliest dog in the world. It can kill any dog in a fight." The customer replied, "Your dog isn't *the* deadliest. I have a long-tailed, short-legged, long-nosed, short-haired terrier that is the toughest animal alive." So the bartender sees a challenge and says, "I'll bet you $100 that my bull mastiff can kill your long-tailed, short-legged, long-nosed, short-haired terrier." The customer takes him on, and says he's going to get the dog and bring it back. Sure enough, the customer brings back the dog and the fight begins. The long-tailed, short-legged, long-nosed, short-haired terrier takes one bite of the huge bull mastiff and the big brute disappears! The bartender says in disbelief, "Are you sure that is a long-tailed, short-legged, long-nosed, short-haired terrier?" The customer says, "Yes, its a crocodile terrier!"

Older man to his friend.

"You know you've got to be ready, willing, and able. Two out of three won't work!"

* * *

Pinkus is in his office, working late on a dismal winter day. He calls his wife to tell her he'll be home late. At around 10 P.M. he goes to a Chinese restaurant and the waiter is working hard, serving course after course, singing and humming. Pinkus, who at this point is chilled, tired, and hungry, asks the waiter what there is to be so happy about. The waiter replies, "I'm thinking of my sex life." Pinkus asks, "What's so special and wonderful about your sex life?" The waiter responds, smiling, "I take my time with sex. I put it in, I say, 'Excuse me,' I take it out, I go to the kitchen and drink a glass of rice wine." Pinkus thinks this is interesting but doesn't really see it as a cause for such happiness on such a miserable working day. He asks the Chinaman again, "So that's all that's special about your sex life?" The Chinaman replies, "That's right. I just take my time. I put it in, I say, 'Excuse me,' I take it out, I get a little refreshment, I go back and put it in, and I have a wonderful time."

When Pinkus goes home that night, he decides to give the waiter's routine a try. He's making love to his wife, he puts it in, says, "Excuse me, I'm going to get a glass of Manischewitz." He returns, puts it back in, after a while takes it out, and says, "Excuse me, darling, I'm going to get a knish." At that point, his wife pipes up and says, "You know, Pinkus . . . you fuck just like a Chinaman!"

Pinkus is in Las Vegas, gambling. He's lost all his money, and is waiting for his banker to wire him some more. He's on his way up to his hotel room when he sees a beautiful hooker in the elevator. He falls in love with her right on the spot, and tells her, "I want you, I'm in love with you, I want to make love right now!" The hooker says, "That's nice. If you've got the cash, we'll go." Pinkus replies, "Ahhh ... I'm broke. I'm waiting for my banker to wire me some money." The hooker shakes her head and says, "No money, no go, buddy." Pinkus replies, "But honey, I'm wild about you. You drive me nuts." The hooker says, "I can see that by the bulge in your pants." So she does him a favor. She takes out his penis and writes, "GLORIA, 357-6262 when you have $$." He returns to his room, and a couple of hours later, the wire comes in. He immediately rushes over to the telephone, ready to call his dream woman. One of his friends comes out of the bathroom and sees him by the phone, fiddling with his fly. He says to Pinkus, "What are you doing, fiddling with your fly, a man of your age?" Pinkus says, "Would you believe trying to make a phone call!"

* * *

A man walks into the ladies' room by mistake, and the first woman who sees him starts to scream. He says to her, "Shhh, madam, don't scream." The woman says, "But this is for women only!" And he says, pointing to his dick, "So is this!"

* * *

Johnny came home from his office. He was terribly disheveled. His hair was a mess, his fly down, his shirt torn, and there were lipstick smudges all over the front of his pants. His wife asked, "Did you have a hard day at the office?" Johnny said, "It wasn't too bad. I got a new secretary, but I think she'll do very well." His wife asked, "Does she take shorthand?" Johnny exclaimed, "No, she gives it!"

* * *

Ralph unexpectedly came home for lunch, only to find his wife lying in bed naked with large hickies all over her neck and big red bruises and red welts all around her tits, where she had obviously been ravaged in sexual passion. Then he noticed a burning cigar on the nightstand next to the bed. Ralph screamed, "Who's been sucking on your tits?" His wife answered, "No one, Ralph. Whenever I try to smoke a cigar I break out in a rash!"

* * *

Jon says to his friend, "Albert, do you like women with big breasts?"
Albert says, "No!"
"Albert, do you like women with big fat asses?"
Albert says, "No!"
Jon then says, "Then why are you fucking my wife?"

* * *

Did you hear about the old lady who's afraid of flies?
Until she opened one!

All these sperm are hanging around. Stanley the sperm is working out, swimming laps and lifting weights. Everyone else is just lounging around. The other sperm say, "Stanley, what are you working out for?"

Stanley says, "When the time comes, I want to be the one."

The other sperm say, "What are the chances of that, one in a million?"

The time comes, and they all start swimming and Stanley is way ahead of them. Then all of a sudden Stanley stops and starts swimming backward and tells everyone to turn around and go back.

Everybody says, "Stanley, what's the matter?"

Stanley says, "It's a blow-job."

* * *

Jack goes into this bar and the bartender says to him, "I've never seen you around here before." And Jack says to him, "Are you kidding? Everybody knows me. I'll bet you $100 that everybody here knows me." Jack walks over to a bunch of people standing at the bar and everybody says, "Hey, Jack, how are you doing?" The bartender can't believe it; he's never seen Jack before. Jack says, "I bet everybody in this country knows me. I'll bet you $500." Jack and the bartender go to Washington, D.C., and pay a visit to the President. The President comes out and says, "Hey, Jack, how are you?" The bartender can't believe it. Jack says, "I'll bet everybody in the world knows me. I bet you $1,000!" Jack and the bartender go to the Vatican. Jack goes to see the Pope, and Jack and the Pope come out and stand at the window. All of a sudden there is a big commotion down below and an ambulance pulls up. Jack comes down to see what's wrong and it's the bartender — he's fainted. When he comes to, the bartender says, "I watched everybody in the bar recognize you, and I watched the President recognize you, but when the guy next to me said, 'Who's that guy with Jack?' that was more than I could take!"

* * *

An old man and woman are sitting on their porch, rocking back and forth on rocking chairs. The man says to the woman, "Fuck you!" The woman says, "Fuck you!" The man: "Fuck you!" The woman: "Fuck you!" The man: "Fuck you!" The woman: "Fuck you!" The man says to the woman, "You know, this oral sex ain't all its cracked up to be."

* * *

Why was the sailor covered with sand?
  He was blown under the pier by a Wave!

* * *

What does a man after an orgasm have in common with the girl he's on top of?
  They both want to get off!

* * *

Show me a man who has bought one of those new Ferraris, and I'll show you a happy man — the salesman!

Those new little sports cars are weird. In order to cross the street now, you have to look right, left, and down!

* * *

"Bill, between you and me, isn't love silly?"
"Fred, between you and me, it would be absurd!"

* * *

I knew a woman that was fucked so much they called her the Iron Maiden.

* * *

What's the definition of a successful marriage?
That's when the housekeeper and the wife come a couple of times a week!

* * *

The Beatles . . . remember them?
Well, they wouldn't remember you!

* * *

As a small child, I couldn't understand why so many people flipped out!
As an adult, I can't understand why everybody doesn't flip out!

* * *

A father is walking past his son's room, and hears his son praying, "God bless Mommy and Daddy and please take care of Grandpa when he comes to visit you tomorrow." And the father thinks, hmmm, but doesn't say anything. The next day Grandpa dies and the father thinks about his son's prayer the night before, but doesn't say anything. So the next night, the father is walking past his son's room again and hears him saying his prayers. "God bless Mommy and Daddy, and please take care of Grandma when she comes to visit tomorrow." Sure enough, the next day Grandma dies.

The father is very upset about this, but doesn't say anything. He passes by his son's room once again, and hears him saying his prayers. "God bless Mommy, and please take care of Daddy when he comes to visit tomorrow." So the next day the father takes everything real slow. He's very cautious, looks both ways before he crosses the street, and remains acutely aware of everything happening around him. He comes home that night, and his wife says, "Gosh, you look horrible. Did you have a bad day?" He says, "Yes, but everything is O.K. now. I'm home." The wife says, "Well, I had a bad day today. The milkman had a heart attack and died right here on the kitchen floor!"

* * *

A farmer has a pet parrot who constantly fucks the chicken in the chicken coop. The farmer tells the bird, "Stop fucking the chicken or I'm gonna get you out of there." The farmer goes out again and comes back, and sure enough, the parrot is fucking the chicken again. The farmer threatens, "I'm gonna give you one more chance. If you fuck my chicken one more time, I'm gonna shave your head." Once again the farmer goes about his other chores but returns later to the chicken coop to find the parrot at it again with the chicken. This time, true to his word, he shaves the parrot's head.

The farmer decides to have a party. During the party, the parrot's job is to tell all the ladies to go to the left, and all the men to go to the right, as they enter the party. The parrot is directing the activity from the back of the room, on top of the piano. "Good evening, miss. Please step to the right." "Hello, sir, to the left, please." When a bald man walks in the door, he says, "And you, chicken fucker, come to me on the piano!" The farmer gets so upset with the parrot for saying this to his guest that he sends the parrot to his brother in the city. The brother warns the parrot, "You'd better be a good bird. My brother told me all about you and your nasty habits, and let's get it straight right now. I don't want any trouble." So before the brother leaves for work one morning he orders two tons of coal for the winter.

When he returns in the evening, he discovers that twice the amount of coal has been delivered. He decides to keep the extra coal, just in case it's very cold. The next day when he returns from work, he notices that again another shipment of coal has been delivered. This time he calls the coal company and discovers that someone has called from his home and doubled the original order and then ordered a second shipment. The brother decides that the parrot is the culprit who mimicked his voice and ordered the extra coal. He decides to nail the parrot's wing up against the wall as punishment. Nailed to the wall, the parrot sees the crucifix up against the wall in the same situation. The parrot says to the crucifix, "Hi, IMVI, did you order coal as well?"

The brother overhears the comment and is so disgusted that he decides to send the bird back to his brother in the country, where he came from. The parrot arrives at the original brother's house, and automatically starts fucking the chicken. At this point, the brother gives up trying to control the parrot's sex habits and lets him fuck the chicken. But one day he comes back and sees that the parrot is dead, lying in the middle of the field with vultures circling above him, ready to eat him. He can't believe that this parrot has bitten the dust, probably from fucking himself to death. The farmer goes over to the parrot to give him a decent burial and is about to pick him up, when the parrot winks at him and says, "Stop! You're going to ruin my next adventure!"

* * *

Richard Nixon, Gary Hart, and Jimmy Carter were on a fishing trip. The boat started to sink because there were too many people on board. Jimmy Carter yelled out, "Women and children first." Richard Nixon immediately exclaimed, "Fuck 'em." Gary Hart said, "Do we have time?"

* * *

Where's the beef?
 In the Rice.

* * *

What do they call the Gary Hart scandal?
 Tailgate!

Did you hear that when Gary Hart's water bed broke, it was a Rice paddy?

* * *

Gary Hart has changed his position on women's issues. He likes being on top.

* * *

There once was a man named Green,
　Who invented the jerk-off machine.
On the ninety-ninth stroke,
　The fucking thing broke,
　　and smashed his balls to a cream.

* * *

Saint Peter is up at the gate, checking people in. He starts feeling ill and then sees Jesus. He asks Jesus if he will take over for him for an hour. Jesus says, "OK, what do I have to do?" Saint Peter says, "Just get their names and occupations." So Jesus starts checking people in. After a while this one guy comes up and Jesus asks him his name. The man says, "Joseph." And then Jesus asks him his occupation and he says, "Carpenter!" And then Jesus asks, "Did you have a son?" And the carpenter says, "Yes!" And Jesus asks him what he looked like. And Joseph says, "He had nails in his feet and nails in his hands." And Jesus looks at him in amazement and says, "Father?" And Joseph says, "Pinocchio?"

You help a man in trouble and he'll never forget you. Never. Especially the next time he's in trouble.

* * *

Never be led astray into the paths of virtue.

* * *

I am Nefertiti, Queen of the Desert. I can't give you rubies or gold or silver or furs, but if you ever need my sand...

* * *

A debt-plagued fellow, hopelessly poring over a pile of bills, suddenly shouted, "I'd give $1,000 to anyone who would do my worrying for me."

"You're on," answered his wife. "Where's the thousand?"

"That's your first worry," he replied.

* * *

"Hey, Sally," said the college man, "how come you're not wearing my fraternity pin?"

"But, Bob, it was such a nuisance," the pretty coed pouted playfully. "All the fellows were complaining that it scratched their hands."

* * *

Johnny, the stand-up comic, to a heckler in the audience:

"Friend, I need you like newlyweds need the late show."

John was so in love with Jane, and she told him, "I need you like Red China needs Metrical."

* * *

People who give up smoking are like people spending their first day at a nudist camp — what to do with their hands!

* * *

We're prepared to give the common man what he wants — a common woman.

* * *

Women destroy their femininity by a million manly acts.

* * *

Most women today look at marriage as a courtship to the courtroom.

* * *

There are some women that you either leave or kill; loving them is impossible.

* * *

The basic trouble with most women is most men.

* * *

People who got married once create a farce; twice, a tragedy; thrice, insanity.

This prostitute was after a man with a very big penis, and the man with the largest penis lived way out in the desert. So she saved up a lot of money and finally made it out to the desert location. There was a little tent there with an old man inside. She looked at the old man and thought to herself that she had spent all this money to come here. She said to the old man, "I heard that you were the best," and he said, "Yes, ma'am, that's me." She said, "May I see your penis? And the old man showed it to her, and it was only two inches long. She said, "I heard you had a very big penis. He said, "What would you like? Twelve inches?" She said, "Yes!" So he said, "OK!" And clapped his hands twice and, bingo, a twelve-inch penis appeared. Then she said, "Can you make it smaller? Nine inches?" The old man said, "Yes!" And he snapped his fingers twice and the penis went down to nine inches. She said, "Can you make it go up again?" And he said, "Yes!" and clapped his hands twice and it went up again. She said, "Can you make it six inches?" And he said, "Yes!" And he snapped his fingers twice. She thought, wow, this is great, but he's so old. He said to her, "Come here," and told her to get on top of him. He then proceeded to snap his fingers, clap his hands, snap his fingers, clap his hands, on and on!

* * *

What's the definition of marriage?
A three-ring circus with only two people in it.

My wife understands me too well. That's my problem.

* * *

Some people hate each other enough to marry.

* * *

Getting married gave me a lot of insights into life I could do without.

* * *

Jeff was in love with a beautiful girl that he wanted to screw very badly, but he was embarrassed by his small penis and he was afraid to bring up the question, and more afraid of the humiliation of her seeing him naked. One very dark night he picked her up in his car and drove her to a local parking spot. He parked in a very secluded and dark area away from all lights. As he kissed her, he very carefully opened his fly and put his penis in her hand. She said, "Thanks, Jeff, but I don't smoke!"

* * *

Roland, an Australian farmer's son, said, "Father, you were a sheep herder in your younger days, so I was wondering if you could tell me where virgin wool comes from?"

"Son, virgin wool comes from the sheep the herders couldn't touch!"

A man comes home from work and finds his wife sliding down the banister naked. He says, "Darling, what are you doing!" She says, "Warming dinner!"

* * *

A woman goes to a pet store, and she tells the manager that she's lonely and wants a pet and would like his advice in this regard. The man says, "How about this frog?" The woman says, "Why would I want a slimy frog?" The man says, "This frog performs cunnilingus." The woman buys the frog and goes home. She gets naked and the frog gets in bed with her, but nothing happens and she's infuriated. She storms back to the pet shop and complains to the pet store manager. The manager whispers to the frog, "Am I going to have to show you one more time!"

* * *

A husband comes home to his wife, kisses her, and says, "Sweetie, you smell sexy. Is that perfume My Sin?"
The wife says, "No, it's my pussy!"

Part Two

FOOD JOKES

THE WORST DIET YOU EVER READ!

FIVE REASONS WHY YOU DON'T WANT TO BE AN EGG:
1. You only get laid once.
2. It takes five minutes to get hard.
3. You only get eaten once.
4. You have to stay in a box with eleven other guys.
5. The only one who sits on your face is your mother!

* * *

This guy was out of a job and he was looking through the classifieds and saw an advertisement for a bus driver. He thought to himself, "I can drive a bus!" He got the job of driving the Sesame Street bus. On his first day on the job he stopped and picked up his first passengers who were two girls that were extremely fat and a special boy. They got on the bus and one girl said, "Hi, I'm Patty!" The boy said, "Hi, I'm Ross." The other girl said, "Hi, I'm Nester Cheese!" The driver said, "Hi, Nester Cheese!" The driver then looked in his rearview mirror and saw Nester Cheese picking her bunions. The driver couldn't take it anymore. He let everybody out of the bus and went back to the depot and quit. The boss couldn't figure out why he wanted to quit and the driver said, "It's my first day and I had two obese Pattys, special Ross, with Nester Cheese pickin' bunions on the Sesame Street bus!"

* * *

Two missionaries are caught by savage pygmies and thrown into a pot of boiling water. A few minutes later one of the missionaries starts giggling. The other missionary says, "What the hell are you giggling about at a time like this?" The first missionary says, "I just peed."

* * *

A guy wants to kill his wife, and he goes up to another guy named Ardie and says, "Ardie, I can't stand my wife; I've got to have her killed, but all I can afford is a dollar. Will you please kill her for a dollar?" Ardie takes the dollar and follows the wife to the grocery store. Ardie looks around and doesn't see anybody watching, so he sneaks up behind the wife and chokes her to death. Ardie turns around and sees the manager. He thinks the manager has seen him kill the wife so he thinks to himself that he has to now kill the manager. So he goes over to the manager and chokes the manager to death. The headline on the paper the next day reads: "ARDIE CHOKES TWO FOR A DOLLAR AT SHOPRITE!"

* * *

Why do truck drivers make good lovers?
 They know where to eat!

* * *

An inventor introduces a new product to a friend by handing him an apple and telling him to take a bite out of it. The man bites the apple and says, "Oh, my God, it tastes like a peach." The inventor says, "Turn the apple around, and take another bite." The mans says, "Oh, my God, it tastes like a banana. This is unbelievable, but if you could make one of these taste like a cunt, you'd really have something."

A few days later, the two men meet again. The inventor says, "Remember what you told me last week? Try this apple." So the friend bites into the apple, spits it out, and says, "It's horrible. It tastes like shit!" The inventor says, "Well, turn it around to the other side."

* * *

What's moist and pink and split right down the middle?
 A grapefruit!

May the bird of paradise drink the slush out of your earmuff!

* * *

I knew an author whose prose was so sleazy that his writing read like it was dipped in chicken fat.

* * *

I was drinking from a bottle, and it read: "If not satisfied, just return the unused portion of the bottle, and we will cheerfully refund the unused portion of your money."

* * *

My wife cooked her first dinner for me. It was so good I choked on a bone in the chocolate pudding!

* * *

No matter how tough my wife's meat is, I can always count on sticking my fork in her gravy.

* * *

I'd rather have lobsters on my piano . . . than crabs on my organ!

* * *

Tums spelled backwards is SMUT!

You can look at a bulldog and understand why some animals eat their young!

* * *

I invited one of my girlfriends over for dinner, and she was so heavy, when she said she wanted a salad, I put oil and vinegar on the lawn and told her to graze! This same girl got so heavy that once a month they shoved her through the Holland Tunnel to clean it!

* * *

I knew a man who was so stupid he never understood the meaning of the word *plural*. He would order milk, a cookie, and a cookie. Don Rickles would have loved him.

* * *

I knew a girl who was so thin she wore suspenders to hold up her girdle!

* * *

I had a girlfriend once that was so weird she looked like a passport photo for an artichoke!

* * *

I knew a girl they used to call "Miss Soda." She would date anybody from Seven Up!

Oscar Wilde said ignorance is like a delicate exotic fruit. Touch it, and the bloom is gone!

* * *

I knew this girl who changed overnight from a dream boat to a tugboat!

* * *

What do you call a fat girl in shorts?
Stern reality!

* * *

A man breaks wind at a dinner party, and the man near him says, "How dare you break wind before my wife!" The first man says, "I'm terribly sorry. I didn't know it was her turn!"

* * *

I was in a really weird pizza joint. The lights were turned down so low, you could see the mold on the yeast glowing!

* * *

I was very horny one night and went out to a brothel, and I was in one room and the prostitute next to me must have been screwing a candy bar. The entire time I was in there I heard her screaming, "Oh Henry! Oh Henry!"

Do you know what a tiger is?
That's a four-hundred-pound pussy that eats you!

* * *

What's two nuts on a wall?
Walnuts?
What's two nuts on a chest?
Chestnuts!
What's two nuts on a chin?
A blow-job!

* * *

What's a nursery special?
Four and twenty blackbirds baked in a pie. Actually, they couldn't swing it — they trapped fourteen fruit flies in a cheese Danish.

* * *

The young couple was so successful in their new business they were pleased to announce: "We are closing our doors to the public and to all private parties. We're quitting business . . . before we go bananas.

* * *

What do Gary Hart and Prime Minister Nakasone have in common?
They both like to eat rice!

They say a wedding night is just like Thanksgiving! There's a little thigh and leg, lots of breast, but usually an awful lot of stuffing!

* * *

Did you ever notice that black people wear white gloves? Do you know why? So they won't bite off the ends of their fingers when they eat Tootsie Rolls!

* * *

I met this girl who had so many martinis at a party that when she lost her virginity in the back seat of a Rolls-Royce limousine, her drunken lover said, "Well, honey, you lost your olive!"

* * *

Did you hear about the young boy who was thrown out of the Boy Scouts for eating brownies!

* * *

A man was at a plush Caribbean hotel and ordered a drink. The waitress was serving him his martini and said, "Here's something new, an ice cube with a hole in it!" The man said, "What's so new about that? I married one!"

* * *

When President Carter was President, all the hookers in Washington, D.C., left because they couldn't work for peanuts. The hookers came back when Reagan was elected, but now they are leaving again because, how are they supposed to live on peanuts?

* * *

Did you hear about the new protein powder that you can mix in any liquid, and it gives you a hard-on? It works so fast that if you don't swallow quickly it will give you a stiff neck!

* * *

Did you hear about the new psychedelic laxative?
It's a combination prune juice and LSD and makes a regular weirdo out of you!

* * *

Be healthy — eat your honey!

* * *

I'm on a seafood diet. I see food and I eat it!

* * *

Do you know what kind of coffee Marie Antoinette like to drink the most?
Decapitated!

Part Three

HOLLYWEIRD

Jokes about Hollywood, Los Angeles, and the Entertainment Industry

What do you call illegible writing?
　Script tease!

* * *

There was this composer in Hollywood who was so stupid that on his first day at the studio, they brought him sheet music and he connected the dots!

* * *

If God had wanted us to watch television, he would have given us square eyeballs!

* * *

What no wife or writer can understand is that a writer is working when he's staring out the window.

I knew this producer who took a taxi to bankruptcy court, and then invited the driver in as a creditor!

* * *

HOW AN ACTOR CAN GET A JOB
BY THINKING POSITIVELY

Did you know that millions of people only realize ten percent of their capacity for leadership and success in their work because they are shy and lack self-confidence? Does this mean you? Do you cringe and snivel and have silly feelings of inferiority when you meet people merely because they are physically and mentally superior to you?

Of course you do! If you had anything on the ball you wouldn't be reading this type of book.

I can help you. I can show you how to get rid of that lousy personality and change your whole life. A few years ago I met a young man who was so shy that whenever he had a business meeting with an important studio executive or a date with a glamorous movie star he would be unable to think of anything to say and would sit nervously twisting buttons off his clothing (or theirs) and chipping pieces from the furniture with a small hatchet which he carried about for that purpose.

* * *

Lincoln — the man, the car, the biography, the miniseries, and the tunnel!

A Hollywood author wanted to call his book "How to Make a Million Dollars and Speak Correct English and Be Good-Looking and Sexy and Healthy and Well Read and Perfectly Groomed and What Wines to Order with What Meals and Write Popular Music and Learn Taxidermy in Your Spare Time." He couldn't use it, though. There was already another book by that name!

* * *

One of the worst things that can happen to an actor is to meet someone at a party and have them say, "I remember your name. I just can't place your face!"

* * *

"Ladies and gentleman, boys and girls, today we are going to present the first episode of a children's edition of 'The Dating Game.' We have three extremely handsome young teenage boys who cannot be seen by our teenage girl contestant. The girl is petite, fourteen-year-old Robin Banks from Wildwood, N.J. Now Robin, would you be kind enough to begin the questioning?" Robin says, "Contestant number one, my first question is, how big is your dick?"

* * *

I knew this really stupid prostitute in Hollywood. She thought Moby Dick was a social disease!

Did you hear that Dean Martin moved to Alcatraz? He always wanted a house on the rocks, with a little water on the side!

* * *

What's a country-western ten?
A four-wheel drive pickup truck and a six-pack.

* * *

A filmmaker dies and goes to heaven. When he's there, he meets Saint Peter. Saint Peter says, "I'm glad you're here. We're going to go immediately into the film business. The filmmaker says, "I'm in heaven, Saint Peter. I'm not interested in the film business anymore. I want nothing to do with it!" Saint Peter says, "Well, we've got Shakespeare to write the screenplay." The filmmaker shakes his head. "I'm definitely not interested in the movie business." Saint Peter says, "Well, we've got Mozart to write the score." The filmmaker says, "I'm still not interested." "Well, we've got James Cagney to star in it," says Saint Peter. The filmmaker says, "Oh, my God! You have James Cagney! Well, I guess it's a go." Saint Peter says, "Well, there's just one more thing I have to tell you. God's got this girlfriend who sings!"

* * *

Johnny Lyons, a well-known Hollywood theatrical agent, discovered that one of his most beautiful actresses was acting as a prostitute and selling her services for $200 to $400 a shot. Johnny, who wanted to plug her himself, was astounded that she was a whore. So he finally approached her and told her that he wanted her bad. She agreed to spend the night with him but insisted that he pay, just like all the rest. Johnny was bewildered by this and suggested that he at least get his commission deducted. The actress refused and Johnny accepted.

Later on in the evening, after the actress completed a singing performance at a Hollywood hot spot, she came to her agent's apartment and he screwed her around 12:30 A.M. for the first time and turned out the lights. At 1:30 A.M. she was awakened again, and they screwed again. In a little while she was awakened again and was screwed once more. The actress was extremely impressed with her lover's virility. "Oh, my gracious," she whispered in the dark into his ear, "I never realized how fortunate I was to have such a sexually charged agent." "I'm not your agent, lady. He's at the door selling tickets!"

* * *

Did you hear what Donald Duck said to the prostitute?
"Put it on my bill!"

* * *

People in Hollywood have called Johnny Lyons "The Thief of Badgags."

* * *

Jane is so old-fashioned that her idea of exercise is buying an old Bobby Darin record and helping him snap fingers.

Harry, a fairly well-known L.A. television actor, was about to go to the set, but was drunk and needed to sober up immediately. Normally, he would drink coffee, but that would take too long. However, the studio doctor came to the rescue and recommended a coffee enema as a fail-safe method. Harry agreed. The doctor's nurse was performing the enema and Harry yelled, "What brand of coffee are you using?" The nurse replied, "Chock Full O' Nuts!" Harry said, "Stop it, it's the only brand of coffee I hate!"

* * *

Medicine has become so advanced in Hollywood that one surgeon is practicing turning well-used starlets into virgins again. He promised one starlet she would be a virgin again and that he would transform her by taking a small piece of her ear and attaching it to her pussy. The surgery was a complete failure, but something positive materialized in that she could now hear herself coming.

* * *

A well-known Hollywood actor playing Captain Hook for the first time killed himself on the set. Do you know how? He wiped himself with the wrong hand!

* * *

You've heard of the old Hollywood casting couch. Well, this one actress disliked fucking one producer so much that she always did it with her eyes closed. She couldn't bear to see him smile.

Two producers were sitting in a studio screening room viewing the latest production, and one said to the other, "It needs a little cutting!" The other said, "Yes, right down the middle, and be sure to throw both halves away!"

* * *

A typical conversation between an aggressive screenwriter and an arrogant producer on a set in Hollywood might go like this:
The producer would say, "From now on whenever you talk to me keep your mouth shut!"

* * *

I've screwed myself out of fortunes! Most men screw themselves into them.
                                        W. C. Fields

* * *

Do you know the name of the Mexican character who replaced Leonard Nimoy in "Star Trek?"
Mr. Spick!

* * *

What's white and comes in young teenage girls?
Roman Polanski!

* * *

Did you hear that Joan Collins has been voted "Woman Chef of the Year"?
She's got more meat between her legs than any other cook!

Do you know why Joan Collins was voted the most popular girl by the Canadian Mounted Police?

Because she'd been mounted more than any horse in the entire herd.

* * *

The level of cultural sophistication in L.A. is very high. Whenever anyone mentions art, someone says, "Art who?"

Part Four

ETHNIC JOKES

Black Jokes

A black man dies, and when he gets to the gates of heaven, Saint Peter says, "Excuse me, we do not allow black people in heaven unless they've done a great deed." The black man says, "But I done a great deed. Let me tell you about the great deed I done. I done fucked the daughter of the Imperial Wizard of the Ku Klux Klan at halftime under the bleachers at the Georgia-Alabama football game." Saint Peter says, "Wow, that is a good deed. Tell me, how long ago did you do this?" The black man replies, "Oh, about five minutes ago!"

* * *

Do you know what "fe fi fo, fi fi fo fo" is?
　Larry Holmes' phone number!

A social worker visits a black woman named Mrs. Smith and asks, "How many children do you have?" She answers, "Twelve!" The social worker asks, "How many boys and how many girls?" Mrs. Smith says, "All boys!" The social worker asks, "What are their names?" Mrs. Smith answers, "They all named Dwayne!" The social worker says, "Isn't that confusing? How do you call them individually?" Mrs. Smith says, "Easy, I just calls them by their last names!"

* * *

When do blacks become niggers?
   When they leave the room.

* * *

What's white, weighs sixteen ounces, and is worth $25,000?
   Dwight Gooden's rosin bag!

* * *

What do you call a black priest?
   Holy Shit!

* * *

Will the real Wilt Chamberlain please sit down.

* * *

A black man was in the men's room of a hotel and started taking a leak. The man in the urinal next to him happened to stare at him and noticed that he had a white penis. The man said, "You should be in Ripley's Believe It or Not. I've never seen or heard of a black man with a white dick before!" The other man said, "I'm not black. I'm a coal miner on my honeymoon!"

* * *

Do you know what you call a black hitchhiker?
  Very unlucky!

* * *

What do you call a raw steak and a black intellectual?
  Very rare.

Gay Jokes

What do you call a gay Japanese?
   Hitachi! (he-touch-ee)

* * *

The good news is that they found Liberace's wallet. The bad news is that your picture was in it!

* * *

Did you hear that Liberace was supposed to live another six weeks? But a gerbil popped out of his asshole and saw its shadow!

* * *

What do you call a gay Israeli?
   A Heblew!

A fairy's the type of guy who likes his vice versa.

* * *

A man is in a cafe when he sees a beautiful blonde sitting at the end of the bar. He goes over and starts making the moves on her, and she says, "Beat it, buddy. I'm a lesbian." "Oh," says the man. "What's new in Beirut?"

* * *

The Roman Empire didn't fall — it was pushed!

* * *

Well, if it isn't Fire Island's answer to Brigitte Bardot.

* * *

Young man, well hung, with beautiful body, is willing to do anything. P.S. If you see this, Bob, don't bother to call. It's only me, Tony.

* * *

Take away my deep voice and my hairy chest and what have you got: Twiggy.

* * *

What's the definition of gay?
A little man of dubious gender.

Well, Bruce, she's sort of a male Tab Hunter.

* * *

Catskill resort at 2 A.M.:
 C: (Bangs on mike head.) You got a girl in that room?
 S: Yeah.
 C: (Effeminately.) Oh, you traitor.

* * *

Did you hear about the confused gay Catholic man who couldn't make up his mind whether or not the Pope was just fabulous or simply divine!

* * *

Did you hear about the gay cat burglar?
 When he couldn't blow the elevator, he decided to go down on the elevator!

* * *

Do you know what lesbians like more than Calvin Klein jeans?
 Billy Jeans!

* * *

Do you think it's better to be born black or gay?
 Black, because you don't have to tell your parents!

* * *

A gay man was shopping in New York's Greenwich Village and peeked into a display window. He noticed an enormous rubber dick, and he wandered inside. The store salesman came over to him, and the gay man pointed over at the big black dick and said, "That's the one I want!" The salesman said, "Would you like me to wrap it or put it in a box?" The gay man said, "Don't do anything with it. I'll eat it right here!"

* * *

Johnny Zero's parents always suspected that their son might be gay, but never confronted him with it. However, they were a bit startled when the dean of his college contacted them and said, "Mr. and Mrs. Zero, I have some good news and some bad news for you about your son Johnny." Mrs. Zero said, "Well, give us the bad news first." The dean did inform them of the bad news, that Johnny was gay, but the good news was that this year he was going to be Homecoming Queen!

* * *

Barbara and Lisa, two rather attractive young college students, went on spring-break vacation to Fort Lauderdale this year. Neither suspected the other as being lesbian. When they went to bed that night they shared the same bed for the first time, and one rolled over and quietly said to the other, "Let me be frank." At exactly that moment the other girl said, "No, let me be Frank. You can be Peter."

* * *

Sergeant James was a little fastidious about his inspection of the barracks, and one day he told all the men in barracks A that they were a fucking disgrace standing there in their dirty underwear. So, unbeknownst to him, Corporal Johnson said, "OK, troops, he wants us to change our shorts. Private Edwards, you change with Private Roberts, and Private Dicks, you change with Private Peters, and everyone in the barracks change shorts with a fellow soldier immediately! That's an order!" Sergeant James returned and saw that all the men were still wearing dirty underwear, and said to the men, "Attention! Corporal Johnson, not only are you and your men a fucking disgrace, but you're a bunch of fucking idiots!"

* * *

George and Bruce were chatting with one another, and George pointed out to Bruce, "You are what you eat, and that's why you're a cunt." Bruce said to George, "You're right, George. You are what you eat. That's why you're a prick!"

* * *

Butch and Gene, two gay men, were living together on fashionable Gay Street in Greenwich Village, New York. Despite the fact that they were monogamous, Butch fell in love with a smart-looking new doctor who opened his new practice on their block. Butch told Gene he'd love to meet him, but he didn't know how. Gene didn't mind and said, "Silly, just get sick and book an appointment to see him tomorrow." So Butch did just that, and the next day he went to see the doctor. When in the office the doctor asked him what his problem was, and Butch told him, "I have terrible pains in the anal area." The doctor told him to take off his clothes and he would examine him. Butch did this happily. The doctor then screamed, "It's obvious you're in pain. You have a dozen roses up you ass." Butch said, "Forget about the roses. Read the card!"

* * *

Do you know why Liberace's girlfriend wouldn't live with him?
    He kept coming home shit-faced!

Italian Jokes

Young girlfriend:	Gioseppe, where's my Gioseppe?
Police Officer:	Was he wearing a coat?
Girlfriend:	Yes!
Police Officer:	I think I saw him running down the street, lickety-split.
Girlfriend:	Oh, no. Not Gioseppe! He may grab the tits, feel the ass, but never lick-e-ty split!

* * *

What's the definition of an Italian virgin?
   A girl that can run faster than her brother!

There's a new Italian sports car being built for the Mafia.
It's all hood!

* * *

Unions are getting a bad name. No wonder they are called brother hoods!

* * *

What are the three times an Italian sees a priest?
1. When he's baptized.
2. When he's married.
3. When he's executed.

* * *

What's the difference between an Italian grandmother and a baby elephant?
About ten pounds!

* * *

What's the definition of Italian foreplay?
"Honey, I'm home!"

* * *

The Jews and the Italians have one thing in common. The Jews own the banks, and the Italians rob them!

Do you know what you call twenty-five fat Italian women in a swimming pool?
 The Bay of Pigs!

* * *

Did you hear about the Italian athlete?
 He won an Olympic gold medal and had it bronzed!

Jewish Jokes

Did you hear about the new disease among Jewish women?
 M.A.I.D.S.!

* * *

A man picks up a woman in a bar. He asks the bartender to buy her a drink and asks him to put a little Spanish fly in her drink, because he likes the girl. The bartender replies, "We don't have any Spanish fly, but we have some Jewish fly." The man says, "OK, put in the Jewish fly." The woman drinks her drink, and then becomes a little tipsy and rubs up against the man and says, "Hey, good-lookin', wanna go shopping?"

What's the difference between a nymphomaniac, a prostitute, and a JAP?

A nymph says, "That's all?" A prostitute says, "That's all!" A JAP says, "Beige, I want to paint the ceiling beige!"

* * *

An old Jewish woman is sitting on the beach and a man walks by and she says, "My, you're awfully pale." And the man says, "As a matter of fact, I am." The woman asks why. The man tells her that he's been in prison. The woman says, "So you're single!"

* * *

Three old Jewish women are sitting on a park bench. A flasher comes by and exposes himself. The first lady has a stroke! The second lady gets a stroke! And the third one . . . her arms are too short!

* * *

How do you drive a Jew crazy?
Put him in a round room and tell him there is a dollar in the corner.

* * *

Did you hear about the rabbi who committed suicide?
He found out the girl he was eating was a pig!

How do you keep a JAP from screwing your brains out?
 Marry her!

Polish Jokes

Do you know why Jesus wasn't born in Poland?
 Because it was impossible to find three wise men and a virgin there!

* * *

Did you hear about the Polish man who went to the grocery store with his pregnant wife?
 They said they had free delivery!

* * *

What do you call a very pretty Polish woman!
 Lucky!

* * *

How do you recognize a Polish house in the neighborhood?
 It's the one with the diving board next to the cesspool!

Did you hear about the Polish gambler?
　He took toilet paper to the crap game!

* * *

Why do Polish men carry quarters with their condoms?
　If they can't come, they call!

* * *

Did you hear about the Polish ice-hockey team?
　They drown during spring training!

* * *

How does a Polack counterfeit two-dollar bills?
　He erases the zeroes off the twenties!

* * *

Do you know why the Polish man stopped taking his wife out?
　He heard she was married!

* * *

Do you know why there aren't any Polish golfers?
　Because they don't know their ass from a hole in the ground!

* * *

How do you break a Polack's finger?
　Hit him in the nose!

What's the last thing Polish people do at a wedding?
  Flush the punch bowl!

* * *

One Polish man said to another, "We're going to send a Polish man to the sun!" The other Polish man said, "But won't he melt?" The first man said, "Don't worry, we'll send him at night!"

* * *

Why do Polish students save pop tops.
  They use them as class rings!

* * *

Do you know why idiots spell polish and Polish the same way?
  Because they don't know shit from Shinola!

* * *

What does a Polish girl do after she sucks cock?
  She spits out the feathers!

* * *

How many Polacks does it take to screw in a light bulb?
  Three. One to hold it, and two to turn the ladder!

* * *

How can you tell a Polack in New York City?
  He's trying to get a piece of the rock!

Did you hear about the Polish man who put Odor Eaters in his shoes?
 He walked one hundred feet and disappeared!

* * *

Did you hear about the Polish van Gogh?
 He cut off his dick!

* * *

What was the Polish gigolo doing in the hen house?
 Trying to pick up a chick!

* * *

How did the Polack kill everyone at the masquerade party?
 He decorated his helicopter like a bird and went to the party as a hummingbird!

* * *

Why did the fifteen-year-old Polish girl stop wearing her training bra?
 The wheels were irritating her armpits.

* * *

Why did the Polish grandmother take birth control pills?
 She didn't want her grandchildren to have children!

Two Polish men and a camel have been walking through the desert for days, and are dying of thirst. Finally they approach an oasis, and the men drink up from the pool, but the camel refrains. One man says, "I have an idea! You hold the camel's head underwater, and I'll suck on his asshole and try to draw water up into his system." The other man holds the camel's head underwater and the other man starts sucking on its asshole like mad. After several minutes the man at the camel's rear yells, "Hey, would you mind raising its head a bit? All I'm getting is mud from the bottom!"

* * *

Two Polacks and an Italian are walking down the street when the Polacks encounter a friend. They introduce Gino to their buddy and, after the introduction, say that he's an Italian, and that he is weird because he has two assholes. The buddy asks, "How do you know that?" The Polacks reply, "Because every time we walk into the bar the bartender says, 'Here comes the Italian with two assholes!'"

* * *

Five Polish guys are standing around shooting up. One guy walks in and says, "Haven't you guys heard about AIDS?" One of the Polacks says, "Yes, we're all wearing rubbers!"

* * *

Did you hear about the Polack who went to Alaska?
He always carried a six-pack in case he had to leave a message in the snow!

How did the Polish soldier die?
  From saluting!

* * *

How do you get a Polack out of the bathtub?
  Fill it with water!

* * *

Did you hear about the Polish woman who thought a sanitary belt was a drink from a sterilized shot glass!

* * *

Do you know how a Polack takes a shower?
  He pees in the fan!

* * *

Did you hear the one about the Polish guy who wore condoms in his ears because he was afraid of hearing aids?

* * *

What's a Polish wedding proposal?
  "You're what?"

* * *

How do you tell the bride at a Polish wedding?
  The one with hair under the arms.
How do you tell the groom?
  The one with the clean bowling shirt.

What's a Polish vacation?
Sitting on your neighbor's back stoop with a six-pack.

* * *

A Polack went to a pizza parlor and ordered a pizza. When the pizza was done, the pizza chef asked how he would like it cut — into four, six, or eight pieces. The Polack said, "Four. I'll never be able to eat more than four pieces!"

* * *

A Polack and an Italian are sitting in a bar watching the eleven o'clock news and watching a woman attempt suicide and the Polack says, "I'll bet you $50 she doesn't jump!" The Italian says, "I'll bet you $50 she does jump!" So they make the bet and a few minutes later the woman does make the jump and plunges to her death. The Polack hands over the $50 and says, "You won." The Italian replies, "I really can't take your money! I saw her do it on the six o'clock news." "Why, I saw the six o'clock news too, and I never thought she'd jump twice!"

* * *

Paul lived in Poland. One day he came home from the glass factory early and found his wife in bed with his friend Rudy, the butcher. They all started screaming! Then Paul ran to his desk, pulled out a pistol, and confronted his wife. He put the pistol directly to his own head and grinned at her. "Don't feel bad for me, you bitch. You're next!"

A Polish man was suffering from severe constipation. He went to his doctor, who prescribed suppositories. A week later the Polish man went to his doctor again and claimed he was still constipated and that the suppositories didn't work. The doctor asked if he had been taking them regularly. The Polish man replied, "What do you think I've been doing, putting them up my ass!"

* * *

Do you know why Polish men have been accused of being such poor lovers?
Because they always wait for the swelling to go down!

* * *

Did you hear about the Polack who stayed up all night to study for his urine test and flunked it!

* * *

Did you hear about the dumb Polish doctor who delivered a stupid baby and was accused of being a dope peddler!

Miscellaneous Ethnic Jokes

What's the definition of a Puerto Rican virgin?
 A woman with only twelve kids!

* * *

Arabs are tense lovers. In fact, they do everything in tents!

* * *

Washington's Birthday is celebrated in every state except Florida. Down there they figure that a man who could not tell a lie isn't worth remembering.

* * *

Russia upped its standard of living and now it is challenging China to do the same — up yours!

The biggest problem in Russia isn't keeping males and females apart, it's telling them apart!

* * *

She's from the twin cities — Sodom and Gomorrah!

* * *

A well-known diplomat attached to the American Embassy in Denmark had just returned from a weekend in the midlands at a stately country home. When he was asked by a friend whether or not he'd had a good time, he said, "If the soup had been as warm as the wine, and the wine as old as the chicken, and the chicken as tender as the upstairs maid, and the maid as willing as the duchess, it would have been perfect."

* * *

Prosperity in Alaska: The Eskimos still drive sleds, but without dogs. They're now pulled by eight Volkswagens.

* * *

An Arab stood on a weighing machine
   In the light of the lingering day.
A counterfeit coin he slipped in the slot
   And silently stole a weigh.

* * *

Did you hear about the Arab who ate his date!

How do you drive an Irishman crazy?
Put him in a round room and tell him there is a bar in the corner.

* * *

Where does a horny Indian couple go?
To the happy humping grounds!

* * *

You look at the news every day; there's rape, muggings, strikes. Maybe the Indians should have had stricter immigration laws.

* * *

"Well," one Indian said to another, "It didn't bring rain, but you've got to admit it was one helluva ceremony!"

* * *

An Indian drank sixty-two cups of tea. The next morning they found him dead in his tea-pee!

* * *

Did you hear about the new Broadway nightclub run by Indians?
They charge $24 for a Manhattan!

* * *

Remember when kids used to run away? Now they defect!

Do you know what you call a fat Puerto Rican?
Spic & Span!

* * *

England has become so decadent that overnight it has gone from a nation of shopkeepers to a nation of top-peepers!

* * *

I'd give my wife another Russian wolf-skin coat except the last time I gave my wife a coat like that, whenever it snowed we had to keep her from chasing sleighs!

* * *

An American is a person who isn't afraid to criticize the President . . . but is always polite to traffic cops.

* * *

America is the country where you buy a lifetime supply of aspirin for a few dollars and use it in two weeks!

* * *

When young women are still teenagers they're like the Virgin Islands. They are fresh and unexplored. From their late teens to their thirties, they are like the Orient — a great place to visit and have a wild, sexy time. From forty on, they are like Australia. You know it's down there, but you don't give a damn!

Why did the huge Texan fall in love with the pygmy woman?

He couldn't help it. He was nuts over her!

* * *

I was watching television Saturday morning and was amazed to see that Yogi Bear was now gay. It was strange. I saw him lay his paw on the table.

* * *

What do you get when you cross a Puerto Rican and a Jew?

You get a super who thinks he owns the place!

* * *

A representative of a small African nation was in Russia, and he happened to watch a game of Russian roulette. Someone would put the barrel of a pistol to another's head and pull the trigger. One of the cylinders in the pistol contained a real bullet. Then a Russian representative visited this small African nation. The African ambassador said, "We would like to show you our version of Russian roulette, and we call it African roulette." The Russian asked, "How do you play it?" The African pointed to six full-bodied, voluptuous women sitting in a circle and said, "Any one of these girls would love to give you a blow-job. Take your pick." The Russian said, "Where's the danger? I'm not threatened at all." The African said to the Russian, "One of the girls is a man-eating cannibal!"

Why do Canadians like to fuck doggy style?
So they both can see the hockey game.

* * *

Two men were hunting in the woods, a Polack and an Italian. All of a sudden a beautiful woman came running through the wood, and the Italian said, "Would I love to eat her!" The Italian was acting all excited, so what did the Polack do? He shot her!

* * *

What do you get when you cross a Polack and a Mexican?
A juvenile delinquent who spray-paints his name on chain-link fences!

* * *

What do you call a Chinese voyeur?
A Peking Tom!

* * *

A Brit, a Polack, and a Puerto Rican were all on the top of the World Trade Center, contemplating suicide. The Brit jumped first and fell quickly to a painless death, the Polack couldn't find his way to the ground, and the Puerto Rican stopped every few floors to spray-paint obscenities on the windows on the way down.

Do you know why there aren't any vampires in India?
A vampire who sucks Indian blood gets the shits for a week.

* * *

What do you call an East Indian dick?
Delhi meat.

* * *

What do you call a hooker from Canada?
A Canadian Mountee.

* * *

What do you call a mixture of a Libyan and a dog?
Nothing? There are some things a dog won't do either.

* * *

What's it called when you cross a Libyan with a gorilla?
A crazy gorilla!

Part Five

CONCEITED LINES

I wouldn't say I stole the act. Let's just say I have a highly creative memory.

* * *

I have a sixth sense — I lack the other five.

* * *

I know he's not two-faced. Otherwise he'd be kissing himself.

* * *

He was so vain that he joined the navy so the world could see him.

He wanted his X-rays retouched.

* * *

On his birthday he sends his mother a telegram of congratulations.

* * *

The great thing about being an egotist is you don't go around talking about other people.

* * *

I just want one single thing in life — myself.

* * *

He wants to be the center of attraction. He goes to a funeral and wants to be the corpse.

* * *

I've given up reading books. I find it takes my mind off myself.

* * *

People say I'm conceited, but that's ridiculous. It's just that I have a fondness for the good things in life, and I happen to be one of them.

* * *

I'm not really conceited. I just have a high opinion of people with ability, good looks, and personality.

He who falls in love with himself will have no rivals.

* * *

I never take a hot shower. It clouds the mirror.

* * *

I had rather men should ask why no statue has been erected in my honor than why one has.

* * *

I had sibling rivalry with my toy robot. I got jealous when it got batteries and I didn't.

* * *

I used to be disgusted. Now I'm amused.

* * *

Since I gave up hope, I feel much better.

* * *

This is no ordinary person you're dealing with.

* * *

If you don't like the way I drive, get off the sidewalk.

* * *

You must be walking backward. All I see is an asshole.

Heaven doesn't want me, and hell's afraid I'm going to take over.

* * *

When I die, bury me upside-down so the whole world can kiss my ass.

Part Six

**VERY SICK AND
EXTREMELY SICK JOKES**

Life is a shit sandwich. . . . The more bread you have, the less shit you eat!

* * *

Humans are better than computers. . . . They're easier to maintain, and can be produced by inexperienced labor!

* * *

Ronald Reagan arrives in hell and he's being shown around the place. When passing a pit of unspeakable slime and filth he saw all the Watergate crew. John Dean was covered to the waist. Haldeman and Erlichman were submerged up to their necks. Next to them John Mitchell was only knee-high in the slime. "Hey," the President said, "how come old Mitch rates such preferential treatment?" "Don't worry about it," said the devil. "He's standing on Nixon's shoulders."

* * *

Newark kids have a problem around Father's Day. . . . It's not what to give. It's who to give it to!

* * *

Definition of a lecture:

A lecture is something that makes you feel numb at one end and dumb at the other!

* * *

What's the sharpest thing in the world?
A fart. It can go through the tightest fabric without making a hole!

* * *

What's the strongest thing in the world?
A piss. Even Superman can't hold it!

* * *

Three dinosaurs were named, "Foot," "Foot-Foot," and "Foot-Foot-Foot." One day Foot told Foot-Foot that he wasn't feeling well. Foot-Foot told Foot-Foot-Foot about Foot's illness, and Foot-Foot-Foot said, "Listen, Foot-Foot. You'd better tell

Foot to take care of himself." A few weeks went by, and Foot was sick again. Foot-Foot passed the news on to Foot-Foot-Foot, who said again to tell Foot to take care of himself. In another two weeks, Foot died. Foot-Foot told Foot-Foot-Foot that Foot died. Foot-Foot-Foot told Foot-Foot that the two of them had better take excellent care of themselves. Another two weeks passed, and Foot-Foot felt sick. Foot-Foot-Foot said to Foot-Foot, "Listen, Foot-Foot, we'd better take care of ourselves. We already have one Foot in the grave!"

* * *

Peter is a young businessman, and Arthur is an older businessman whose offices are in the same building. Arthur barges into Peter's office one day, and when Peter complains, Arthur asks, "What's the matter. Should I knock before I come in here?" Peter says, "No, no! Around here you have carte blanche." Arthur says, "Carte blanche? Can it be cured with penicillin?!"

* * *

An extremely fat, dumpy lady has vaginal pains only during rain- or snowstorms. She tells her girlfriend about the pain, and the friend says, "Don't tell me. Call the doctor. This sounds serious." So the woman visits the doctor, and after a thorough exam, he pronounces her in perfect health. He adds, "If you have the pain again, call me and we'll have you in right away for an exam. So one day during a rainstorm, the woman has the pains again. She calls the doctor from a phone booth, and he tells her to come right down to his office, he'll take a look. She's in the office, feet in the stirrups, with the doctor working away. All at once the pain stops. "Doctor, doctor!" says the woman. "The pain has stopped! What on earth did you do?" The doctor replies, "I cut three inches off your galoshes!"

* * *

I was so ugly when I was born, the doctor slapped my mother!

* * *

I try never to be alone. My mother always told me to avoid bad company.

* * *

I said to my mother-in-law, "My house is your house!"
So what does she do? She sells my house!

* * *

Did you hear about the farmer's daughter?
She was ate before she was seven.

* * *

Did you hear about the British gentleman?
He liked to eat his tomato's hole!

A dog was sitting close to the railroad tracks when a train came by and sheared its tail off. The dog was so mad he chased after the train, and when he caught up with it, he tried to bite it and had its head cut off. The moral to this story is, Never lose your head over a piece of tail!

* * *

What's the definition of gross?
When you go to kiss your grandmother and she slips you the tongue!

* * *

A man has crabs, and his friend advises him to rub sugar all over his balls.
The man says, "Will it kill them?"
The friend says, "No, but it will rot their teeth and stop them from biting you!"

* * *

Johnny takes his date to the cinema, and while they are kissing, his toupee falls off. He's looking around for it, and his hand goes up his girl's skirt. She whispers passionately into his ear, "That's it! That's it!" Johnny says, "It can't be! I part mine on the side!"

* * *

Why was the duchess on her knees?
She was down for the count!

Why does an elephant have four feet?
He'd look pretty silly with six inches!

* * *

The barber says to the man, "Would you like me to wrap your head in a hot towel?" The man says, "No, I'll carry it home under my arm!"

* * *

What's the definition of a toupee?
Ear-to-ear carpeting!

* * *

His mother said that when he grew up, he would come out on top. She was right, and now he's bald!

* * *

A contemporary used-car salesman's pitch has changed. In order to cope with cynical attitudes of present-day buyers, the little old lady who drove only on Sundays has been replaced in a salesman's standard sales pitch by a nymphomaniac who only used the back seat!

* * *

One thing I like about my new Ferrari is that it has great pick-up. Last night I picked up two blondes!

I want you to be careful when you're driving home tonight because ninety-six percent of all people are caused by accidents. Somehow that doesn't sound right. Accurate perhaps — but not right.

* * *

K.I.S.S.
Keep it short, stupid!

* * *

Men who are getting on in years should console themselves with the thought that when they get too old to set bad examples, they can always start giving advice!

* * *

He claims his furniture goes back to Louis XIV, and it will if he doesn't pay Louis before the fourteenth.

* * *

A man is in the desert riding on a camel, and since he's been in the desert for over a year he's become extremely horny. All of a sudden his sexual anxiety gets to him, and he can't take it anymore and he makes a pile of rocks and puts the front of the camel on the top of the rocks so the back of the camel will be lower. The man mounts the camel and the camel immediately takes a step forward. The man puts the camel back on the rocks and attempts to mount it again, and the camel moves forward. The man continues with his advances, to no avail. Then an extremely beautiful woman approaches, and he runs up to her and says, "Ma'am, would you be kind enough to hold my camel?"

* * *

What's dark brown and you only see it once in a while?
Turd cousins!

* * *

I was in a house that needed some refurbishment. It could have used a good coat of fire!

* * *

"Your Majesty, the people are revolting."
"Oh, yeah? You're not so good-looking yourself!"

* * *

We have a wonderful house about ten miles out of town with a 100-by-125-foot lot, and the entire place is surrounded by mortgages. It's a sort of split level but wasn't always a split level. It used to be a ranch house, then the foundation settled. It's the only house where you go upstairs to the cellar.

* * *

I have the only horse in the race with training wheels!

I hired my mother to clean, but I had to let her go. She stole!

* * *

My grandfather on his deathbed sold me this watch!

* * *

I wrote to the Peace Corps the other day, and they wrote back, "Leave us in peace."

* * *

People who have no faults are terrible.
There's no way of taking advantage of them!

* * *

I can resist everything except temptation!

* * *

"Why are your socks on inside out?"
"Well, my feet got hot and I turned the hose!"

* * *

"Did you fill in the blank yet?"
"You mean the one between my ears?"

* * *

I'd be a good dancer except for two things: my feet!

One prisoner said to another, "You're going to spend so much time up the river, you're going to be making eyes at the salmon!"

* * *

One teacher in a very sexually charged classroom put a sign on the wall that said, "My motto is make love, not war, but not during class!"

* * *

The definition of a synonym is: "A word used when you can't spell another word."

* * *

What's the definition of *alas*?
Early Victorian for, Oh, hell!

* * *

No one is purfict!

* * *

I know a man who's sixty-three: He smokes four packs of cigarettes a day. He doesn't mind if it hardens his lungs. At his age, he's glad if anything gets hard!

* * *

What does CUNT stand for?
Can't understand normal thinking!

A good way to kill rats is to pour ground glass in their holes. Of course you have to hold the rats!

* * *

Dr. James was delivering a baby, and the operation was successful. However, the mother, Mrs. Waldo, was extremely upset because her baby was extraordinarily ugly. The doctor said, "Don't worry, ma'am. When I was born, I was so ugly my mother took the placenta home!"

* * *

Did you hear about the guy who got a job working in a pool room cleaning the balls in the backroom after the customers shot!

* * *

What about the guy who worked in the butcher shop who took his meat in the back!

* * *

What about the guy who got a job taking fly shit out of pepper jars with boxing gloves!

* * *

What did Ted Kennedy say to Gary Hart?
"Next time, let me drive her home!"

Did you know Richard Nixon, Gary Hart, and Teddy Kennedy have formed a law firm? It's called Trick 'Em, Dick 'Em, and Dunk 'Em.

* * *

Bud McFarlane said at the end of his testimony on Capitol Hill, "I regret that I have but one lie to give to my country."

* * *

What does an elephant use as a vibrator?
A epileptic!

* * *

I wear glasses and you, sir, are a fright for four eyes.

* * *

She wore a big formal dress with a hoop. I didn't know whether to say, get in the car, or bail out.

* * *

Some people say I'm a no-account; other say I'm a count.

* * *

Vitamins A, D, B . . . Now, why can't I have rickets like all the other kids?

"Why did you buy that?"
"Because I don't have the nerve to steal it."

* * *

"Warden, the prisoners seem very contented."
"Yes. We try to give the prisoners sympathy and understanding . . . along with the constant beatings."

* * *

The world's really strange. Today crazy teenagers drive 90 m.p.h. down the highway kissing and holding hands from different cars, going in opposite directions.

* * *

We were supposed to have another person here, but last week he was called to a "great eternal resting place" — he got a civil service job.

* * *

You're doing a wonderful job. Too bad it's not in this business.

* * *

When you don't have an education, you just have to use your brains.

* * *

There are two schools of thought about me. People either dislike me or hate me.

One person is just like another. Take him — I don't even know him and I hate him already.

* * *

You can't hear? Well, listen louder!

* * *

Want to hear a good gag? (Put finger in throat and make gagging noise.)

* * *

Colleges are really getting rough. They won't give a football player his letter unless he can tell which one it is.

* * *

At first I thought she just had a bad complexion. Then I found out they were harpoon scars.

* * *

Football lineup: halfback, fullback, quarterback, and in his case a drawback.

* * *

When he was born, his mother said, "What'll we call it?" and his father said, "Let's call it quits."

This girl was really ugly. She was in an auto accident and her face caught fire. They put it out with a shovel.

* * *

"How do you do?"
"How do I do what?"

* * *

#1: Just remember these three little words: "Don't argue."
#2: But that's two words.
#1: See, you're starting already.

* * *

S: He has a heart of gold.
C: If he had a heart of gold, he'd have sold it.

* * *

I won't say my boyfriend's cheap, but when he pays his own check, he's treating.

* * *

I'm not cheap. I give till it hurts — but I'm very sensitive to pain.

* * *

I want all the people reading this book to realize that mental illness strikes once every sixty seconds.

Laughing at me is like drop kicking a wounded hummingbird.

* * *

Our new house is terrific! Wall-to-wall carpeting, wall-to-wall air conditioning, back-to-the-wall payments.

* * *

I was caught in the middle of a panty raid — pink-handed.

* * *

I bought two hundred shares of Consolidated Union Suit — and then the bottom fell out.

* * *

The public is wonderfully tolerant. It forgives anything but genius.

* * *

The only thing more expensive than education is ignorance.

* * *

One ant to another:
 "You know what makes me feel sorry for humans?"
 "No, what?"
 "Those big ugly pores."

A plumbing salesman used to say his tubs were the biggest thing in bathtubs since rings.

* * *

My name is Johnny Lyons and I'm an original — only one of its kind in captivity.

* * *

"What's your name?"
"John."
"Downstairs and to the left."

* * *

I was at a wife-swapping party and everyone threw all the keys on the floor. I took one — ever try making love to a Chevrolet?

* * *

At what other time in history do you find people slaving night and day to buy labor-saving devices.

* * *

The building was so high they won't send up an elevator without a weather report.

* * *

He who laughs last laughs best if he can still laugh.

* * *

The best way to get along in today's world is to ignore it.

Have you noticed that people aren't very human anymore? It's too time-consuming.

* * *

Given the state of the world today, it is amazing there is any state at all.

* * *

OK, OK, so I made a mistake and shot and killed her. I said I was sorry.

* * *

My mother-in-law Gilda Rosenberg makes me feel good by doing absolutely nothing; and she makes me feel terrible by doing everything.

* * *

Please! Don't be helpful. I can get into trouble myself.

* * *

Beauty may be only skin deep, but who wants to look underneath?

* * *

Years ago Teddy Roosevelt created the line "Walk softly and carry a big stick." Now it is wise to keep quiet entirely and carry a loaded pistol.

God must be single, because He is so quiet upstairs.

* * *

Money can buy anything but peace of mind, happiness, health, and sanity. Aside from those minor considerations, money is wonderful to have.

* * *

What does an elephant use for a tampon?
A sheep!

* * *

Did you hear about the little girl who swallowed a pin when she was eleven and didn't feel a prick until she was seventeen!

Part Seven

SOME POPULAR SAYINGS

I only sleep with the best!

* * *

I'm not as think as you stoned I am!

* * *

When I'm good I'm very good, but when I'm bad I'm better.

* * *

If you're trying to act like an asshole, you're doing a great job!

* * *

I like your approach. Now let's see your departure!

* * *

Reality is for people who can't handle drugs.

Sex is better than grass, if you've got the right pusher!

* * *

I'm not easy, but we can discuss it!

* * *

Are we having fun yet!

* * *

You're ugly and your mother dresses funny!

* * *

Have a nice day and fuck someone!

* * *

Bend over. I'll drive!

* * *

Talk dirty to me.

* * *

Good girls go to heaven; bad girls go everywhere!

* * *

We'll get along fine as soon as you realize I'm God.

* * *

You've obviously mistaken me for someone who cares!

Sit on a happy face.

* * *

People who think they know it all really annoy those of us who do.

* * *

I've got what you want.

* * *

I don't get mad. I get even.

* * *

Fuck off and die!

* * *

How do you spell relief? D-R-U-G-S.

* * *

I'm number one. Why try harder?

* * *

There are many ways to say I love you, but fucking is the fastest.

* * *

I'm so happy I could shit.

* * *

You are cordially invited to go fuck yourself.

Drugs saved my life!

* * *

I'm not deaf, I'm ignoring you.

* * *

Are you stoned or just stupid?

* * *

Don't fuck with my reality!

* * *

Fuck 'em if they can't take a joke.

* * *

Improve your image; be seen with me.

* * *

I have trouble remembering names. Can I just call you asshole?

* * *

I am the person your mother warned you about.

* * *

I don't need life. I can get high on drugs.

* * *

My karma ran over my dogma.